The Hunt for Rabbit's Galosh

The Hunt for Rabbit's Galosh

By ANN SCHWENINGER

Pictures by KAY CHORAO

DOUBLEDAY & COMPANY, INC.

GARDEN CITY, NEW YORK

ANN SCHWENINGER grew up in Boulder, Colorado. She attended the University of Colorado and graduated from California Institute of the Arts in 1975. *The Hunt for Rabbit's Galosh* is her first book for children. An artist as well as a writer, Ms. Schweninger now lives in New York City.

KAY CHORAO grew up in Cleveland, Ohio, and after graduation from Wheaton College in Norton, Massachusetts, studied at the Chelsea School of Art in London. She is the author-illustrator of *The Repair of Uncle Toe,* and *A Magic Eye for Ha,* and illustrator of *Albert's Toothache* by Barbara Williams and several other books. Mrs. Chorao lives in New York City with her husband Ernesto Chorao, a painter and teacher, and their three young sons.

ISBN 0-385-00130-4 Trade
0-385-00274-2 Prebound
Library of Congress Catalog Card Number 74-33659
Copyright © 1976 text Ann Schweninger
Copyright © 1976 illustrations Kay Chorao
All Rights Reserved
Printed in the United States of America
First Edition

To my parents

RABBIT wiggled his nose. He had mailed a valentine to his mother. Luckily, he got to the mailbox just before it began raining cats and dogs.

Hopping by his desk, Rabbit saw something red. There lay the valentine.

"I'll be a March Hare!" he exclaimed. "I was sure that I had mailed it! Now I'll have to go out in the downpour."

"Here are my coat, hat, gloves, scarf, and umbrella. But where did I leave my galoshes? In the bathroom? Under my bed? In the closet? While I was polishing the banister, I saw one on the stairs — yes! Here it is! But one galosh is no good in a rainstorm. Now where's my other galosh?"

Looking for his other red rubber galosh, Rabbit
bounced into the kitchen. "I left it under the sink!"
Opening the sink door, he cried, "Rooster! I've lost
my galosh. Please help me find it. The sky is like a
river, but I must mail this valentine before the postman
comes."

Rooster crowed, "My aunts and I will search every
corner. We will help you find your rubber boot."

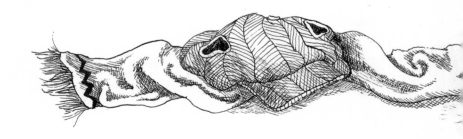

"Wait!" Rabbit exclaimed, "I'm sure I stuck it in the breadbox."

He jumped. "Oh, my ears and tail! Dragon, have you seen my galosh?"

Dragon yawned. Smoke billowed from his nostrils. "No, Rabbit. It's not here, I assure you. There's hardly any room for *me*. Perhaps I will keep an eye out for it, or perhaps I will have a nap." Dragon gave another yawn and blew a puff of smoke.

"Go to sleep before you set fire to the house," said Rabbit. "Rooster and his aunts and I will find my galosh."

He muttered to himself, "In the bookcase? The oven? The china closet? I know!" He leaped to the drawers. "It's with the silverware!"

"Bless my fur! Octopus! I'm in a hurry to mail a valentine. It's pouring torrents and I've lost my galosh."

Octopus waved the teapot. "I have eight arms. I'll feel inside drawers and cupboards, under cushions and behind chairs. I'll find your galosh."

Rabbit smoothed his ears to think. "Wait! It's inside the grandfather clock — how silly of me not to think of it in the first place!"

He skipped to the clock. "Oh, my whiskers! Carrots and rhubarb! Tiger! Is it in there? We've hunted all over the house."

Tiger stretched his stripes. "No, Rabbit, but I'll help search."

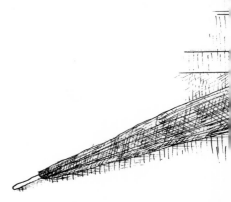

Rooster and the hens cackled and clucked as they peered inside lamp shades, up the chimney, under the rugs.

Octopus felt, all at the same time, under a pillow,
inside a book, behind a picture of Rabbit's uncle, in a
box of carrot chips, along window sills, beneath a
wastebasket, above a chandelier, and around a clothes
hamper. He took a few steps and felt eight more
places. Rabbit hopped to and fro mumbling, "In the
freezer? No. The pantry? The dresser? No."

Tiger roared, "Here it is!" Everyone rushed to him.

"Oh, Tiger," exclaimed Rabbit. "That's my summer hat. We're not looking for a summer hat. Besides, what we're looking for is red."

"Oh," said Tiger, "red?"

Rooster sang cock-a-doodle-do whenever he got a new idea. "Is it in the butter churn?" The hens scratched and peered. Octopus wiggled his arms into every nook and corner.

Rabbit muttered to himself, "In the vacuum cleaner? The bathtub? The hallway? No. May my ears grow longer! Where can it be?"

Tiger growled again, "Here it is!" Everyone rushed to his side.

"No, Tiger," said Rabbit sadly. "That is a mitten."

"But it's red," said Tiger.

"I need it for my *foot*," Rabbit replied.

"Oh," said Tiger, "red, and for your foot!"

Rabbit shouted, "I have it! Inside the piano bench!"

He opened the lid and great wings spread into the room.

"May my garden turn greener! Eagle! Have you seen my galosh?"

Eagle smoothed his feathers. He sharpened his beak on the piano keys, making a little tune. "I haven't, Rabbit, but my eyes are so sharp I can see a mouse at night from a mile in the sky. I'll find it."

Together they all scoured the house. Eagle was first upstairs, downstairs, in the cellar, and in the attic.

Once again Tiger shouted, "Rabbit! Come quick! I've finally found your galosh!"

Rabbit scampered to him. "No, Tiger. That is a stocking."

"But it's red, and you wear it on your foot—"

"It is red, and I wear it on my foot, yes, but it is not rubber. It is not my galosh."

Tiger stammered, "Oh! What—what's a galosh?"

"A rubber boot, Tiger."

"Now I know what to hunt for!"

Rabbit looked out the window. "I was so sure I mailed my valentine," he said. Then he saw the postman coming down the street.

"I'll just have to get my foot wet," cried Rabbit. As fast as he could, he put on his coat, hat, gloves, scarf, and one galosh. He opened his umbrella. He took the valentine for his mother. It was still raining cats and dogs when he went out the front door.

He raced down the street, with one bare foot. And he got to the mailbox, just in time!

THE END